16x
4u: 10/16/99
1/11/2000

11-06

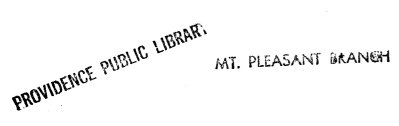

P9-DME-553

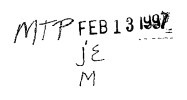
For
Megan, Alexandra, Carla,
Kathryn, Meredith, and Julia

Text copyright © 1996 by Kate McMullan
Pictures copyright © 1996 by Jim McMullan
All rights reserved
Library of Congress catalog card number: 96-85606
Printed in the United States of America
First edition, 1996

When Noel danced, she danced with all her heart.

One Saturday Madam tapped the first place at the barre.
"This," she said, "is where you will stand, Noel."

Noel was so proud to be the leader.

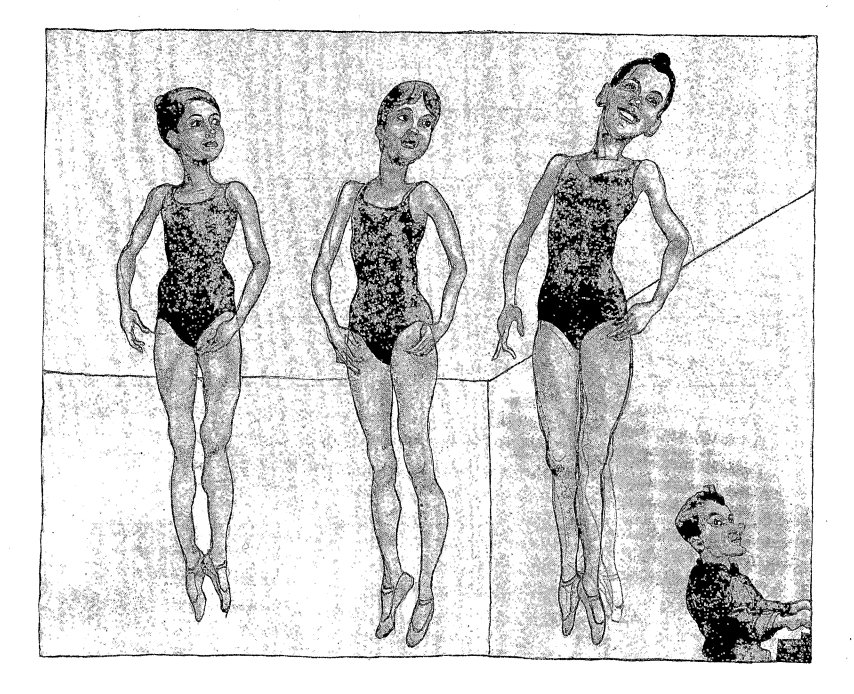

When the class practiced turning and jumping,
Noel was sure she'd never spun so fast or
leaped so high before.

"Noel the First," she thought. "That's me!"

A new girl appeared in the studio one afternoon.
"This," said Madam, "is Anne Marie."

Anne Marie whirled like a whirlwind.
She jumped like a jackrabbit.
Noel couldn't believe her eyes.

"Where did you take ballet before?"
Noel asked her after class.
"Oh," said Anne Marie, "this was my first time *ever*."
"You must be kidding!" said Noel.

"How long have you been taking lessons?"
asked Anne Marie.
"This is my third year," said Noel.
Anne Marie whistled. "Wow! That's a long time."

When Noel got home, she couldn't stop thinking
about Anne Marie.

The very next class, Madam tapped
the first place at the barre.
"This," she said, "is where you will stand, Anne Marie."

When Anne Marie twirled like a twister,
Noel tried to twirl like one, too.

When Anne Marie leaped like a leopard,
Noel tried to leap the same way.
Class after class, Noel the Second
tried to do everything just like Anne Marie.

But Anne Marie stayed first at the barre.

Then one Saturday Anne Marie pranced
into the studio wearing velvet.
"Cool leotard," Noel said.
"This old thing?" said Anne Marie.
"I knew it!" said Noel. "You *did* take ballet before."

"Well," Anne Marie said, "maybe five or six classes."

"I don't think so," said Noel.

"I mean five or six months."

"How long?" said Noel.

"Okay, okay," said Anne Marie. "I've been taking
since I was two."

Just then Madam clapped. Time for class to begin!
But who was this, admiring herself in the mirror?

"This," said Madam, "is Regina Louisa Belinda."

Madam tapped the first place at the barre
and Regina Louisa Belinda stepped right up.
Anne Marie claimed the second spot.
Then came Noel the Third.

That day Madam surprised the girls
by teaching them part of a real ballet.
"This," she said, "is from *Cinderella*.
Two groups, please."

Anne Marie and Regina Louisa Belinda
elbowed their way to the front of the first group.

The music began, and Noel imagined
Cinderella waltzing at the ball.
But Anne Marie and Regina Louisa Belinda
looked more like twin hurricanes ripping up the coast.

When the tune changed, Noel pictured
Cinderella leaping into the Prince's arms.
Anne Marie and Regina Louisa Belinda
looked more like a pair of killer whales
going after the same sardine.

Noel lined up with the second group.
Music filled the studio, and she began
to dance with all her heart,
the way she used to do.

As she let the melody spin her and lift her
and—just for a second—hold her up in the air. . .

Noel turned into Cinderella.

Madam couldn't believe her eyes.
"This," she said, "is dancing!"